Part One

THE SLOBBERERS

The electrifying serial begins...

'I stared. Inside the tin was the little troll that Rory takes everywhere with him. Now it was alive. With worms. They were slobbering all over it and wriggling into the mouth and writhing out of the eyes.'

Dawn and Rory hate each other's guts. And now they are to be step-sister and brother. Even worse, something very weird is happening to the worms Rory keeps as pets.

But what happens when they escape during the wedding is only the beginning. It's what happens next that will **REALLY** make your skin crawl...

It'll suck you in.

Wicked!

Part One

THE SLOBBERERS

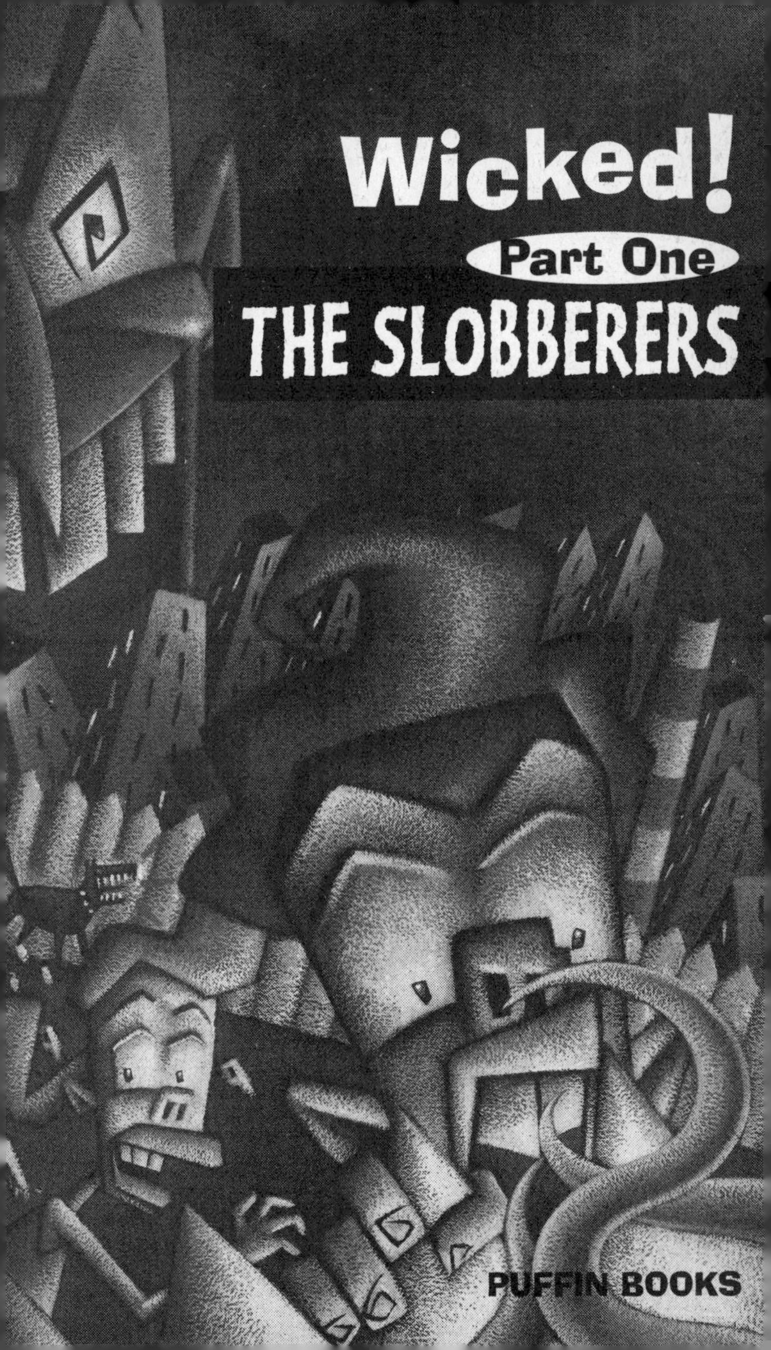

PUFFIN BOOKS

Puffin Books
Penguin Books Australia Ltd
487 Maroondah Highway, PO Box 257
Ringwood, Victoria 3134, Australia
Penguin Books Ltd
Harmondsworth, Middlesex, England
Viking Penguin, A Division of Penguin Books USA Inc.
375 Hudson Street, New York, New York 10014, USA
Penguin Books Canada Limited
10 Alcorn Avenue, Toronto, Ontario, Canada M4V 3B2
Penguin Books (N.Z.) Ltd
Cnr Rosedale and Airborne Roads, Albany, New Zealand

First published by Penguin Books Australia, 1997
10 9 8 7 6 5 4 3 2 1
Copyright © Greenleaves Pty Ltd and Creative Input Pty Ltd, 1997

Typeset in 10/15pt Cheltenham by Midland Typesetters, Maryborough, Victoria
Made and printed in Australia by Australian Print Group, Maryborough, Victoria

National Library of Australia
Cataloguing-in-Publication data:

Jennings, Paul, 1943– .
Wicked!
ISBN 0 14 038775 7 (v.1).

I. Gleitzman, Morris, 1953– .
II. Title.

A823.3

Series editor: Julie Watts
Series designer: George Dale
Cover and text illustrations: Dean Gorissen

THE SLOBBERERS

ONE

They all reckon I'm a worm.

A grub.

A monster.

I could tell from their faces as I ran out of the church. And from what they were saying.

'You're a wicked girl,' hissed Mr Kinloch from the Wool Growers' Association.

I didn't blame him. I'd probably think the same if I saw a kid do what I'd just done. Ruin her own dad's wedding. Leave a church in uproar and a bride in tears and a minister in shock.

I wish Dad had listened all those times I tried to talk to him.

But parents don't listen when love's made them dopey. You

1

just have to go along with their mad plans and hope everyone doesn't end up in the poo.

That's what I was telling myself this arvo in church while Mrs Conti from the cake shop was playing 'Here Comes the Bride' on the organ.

'It'll be okay,' I said in my head as Dad and Eileen stepped up to the altar. 'We can get through this. Dad's a really good dad even though his brain has turned to confetti, and Eileen's not a bad person even though she does dribble a bit when she loses her temper. We'll be right.'

I wanted to believe it heaps. But it was no good. My neck was hurting. I always get neck tension when I try and lie to myself.

I thought a curried-egg sandwich might help. I reached for the one next to me on the pew, the one I'd pinched from the caterers when we'd dropped into the Scout Hall on the way to the church to check that the glitter ball had arrived for the reception.

I hoped the bread hadn't gone too hard in the heat. Rev Arnott's voice was pretty quiet and I didn't want to disrupt the ceremony with crunching. I lifted the sandwich to my mouth.

And froze.

There was a slug sitting on the bread.

Looking at me.

THE SLOBBERERS

It was more of a worm than a slug, slimy and sort of veiny. I'd never seen one like it before, and Dad's a shearer so I've seen lots. You wouldn't believe some of the things that crawl out of sheep's bottoms.

I glared at it and went to knock it off. That's when I saw Rory glaring at *me*.

You'd think grown adults would know better than to put two kids who hate each other side by side on the same pew. Even love-fuddled adults with new shoes that are hurting them a bit should know better than that. But Dad and Eileen were determined.

'She's your step-sister,' Eileen had hissed to Rory when we got to the church. 'Sit next to her.'

'Aw, Mum . . . ' Rory had moaned.

Dad had taken me to one side and given me a pep talk.

'Dawn,' he'd said, squeezing my shoulders. 'I know it's not easy, but we'll all feel more comfortable with each other once we're living together and getting to know each other better.'

I opened my mouth to remind Dad that Rory and me have known each other for eight years and he's hated my guts for five and I've been going off him in a big way for at least four and a half.

Then Mrs Conti deafened us with the organ, and the wedding started.

Two minutes later Rory was grabbing my sandwich.

'That's mine,' I whispered, furious. 'Hands off.'

We struggled over the sandwich.

'The worm's mine,' grunted Rory.

He let go of the sandwich and grabbed the worm.

I chewed my sandwich angrily. How's anyone meant to like a person who keeps worms as pets? Specially when that person's a year older than you and is meant to be setting a good example.

Rory put the worm into a tin.

I stared. Inside the tin was the little troll that Rory takes everywhere with him. The one with the wooden body and the dried apple for a head. I try not to make jokes about it 'cos his dad sent it to him and it's the only present he's had from his dad for ages.

The troll's shrivelled-up apple head had been dry and dead. Now it was alive. With worms. They were slobbering all over it and wriggling into the mouth and writhing out of the eyes.

It was worse than anything I'd seen on a sheep, even in nightmares.

I looked at Rory.

He wasn't gagging or looking revolted or anything. He was staring at the worms, fascinated.

Then I saw something even more horrible.

The tin.

It was *my* tin. My Milo tin. The one Mum had given me to keep pencils in.

I couldn't believe it. Rory had taken it from my room without asking. The last thing Mum had given me before she died. And he'd put slimy slobbery revolting worms in it.

I felt rage uncoiling inside me. Hot tears stinging.

In the distance Rev Arnott was saying that stuff about how if anyone had a reason why these two people should not be joined together in holy matrimony, speak now or forever hold your peace.

Before I knew it I was on my feet.

'I have,' I shouted. I heard the pews creak as everyone stiffened. I could feel everyone's eyes on me.

'We all hate each other,' I said. My heart was pounding in my ears. Dad's mouth was wider than a sheep chute. 'Not Dad and Eileen,' I continued, 'cos they've got sex, but the rest of us.'

Eileen's face was crumpling and Rev Arnott was clinging to the altar. I ploughed on.

'We pretend we like each other, but we don't. You should see Rory go off when I catch him using Dad's razor to scrape the fluff of his socks. You should see Dad when Rory has a nightmare and gets into bed with Eileen. You should see Eileen when I make friendly jokes about her bottom exercises.'

DAWN

'Thank you, Dawn,' croaked Rev Arnott. 'Why don't we finish the ceremony and have a family talk afterwards.'

I turned to appeal to the other guests. Rows of open mouths and big eyes. I pointed at Rory.

'I try to be friendly with him and he lets his rat poo in my underwear drawer.'

'I did not,' shouted Rory. 'It was a mouse.'

'Dawn,' roared Dad, storming towards me, 'sit down.'

'Second marriages never work,' I yelled. 'Specially when she's more educated than he is and her son sneaks into his daughter's room and takes precious things.'

I grabbed at my Milo tin but Rory hung on and the tin spun out of our hands and crashed onto the tiles. The apple head bounced across the floor. Worms slithered everywhere.

I turned and ran out of the church. Dad followed for a bit, shouting, then gave up. I wasn't surprised. Eileen's been more important to him than I have for about a year now.

I suppose I was pretty dopey coming here to the old bus 'cos Dad knows it's where I always come when I want to be close to Mum. When the ceremony's over he'll know where to find me.

In fact I can hear someone crashing through the bush now.

Whoever it is, I'm history.

If it's Dad, he'll kill me for ruining his wedding, and if it's Rev Arnott to tell me I'm forgiven, I've still got to live with Worm Boy.

So either way my life's over.

TWO

Big bad Dawn. Everything is big about her. Big muscles, big head, big mouth and worst of all – big sister. Well, step-sister to be exact. It's not the same. A real sister wouldn't have made a fuss in church over a Milo tin. A real sister wouldn't have nearly let my grubs escape. A real sister wouldn't have ...

Oh, what the heck. I knew where she was hiding.

Everyone from the wedding was looking for her. Fancy standing up in church and objecting to the marriage. What a hoot. I have to give her full marks for that. I wished I'd thought of it myself. I didn't want Mum to marry Jack any more than she did.

The bus. That's where she would be. That was her hideout.

I tucked the Milo tin under one arm and walked along the side of the creek for a while. Then I took the short cut through Dead Cow Clearing. I reached the fence of the wrecker's yard and peered in. There it was. A rusting hulk right in the middle of the yard. Broken windows. Grass sprouting out of the petrol cap. Not a speck of paint left. A tree growing right through the bonnet. And the whole thing leaning drunkenly to one side.

The bus had carried its last passenger, that was one thing for sure.

Last passenger. What was I thinking about? I was the last passenger. I had my crook leg to remind me of that.

I climbed through Dawn's secret hole in the bent iron fence. 'I know you're in there, Dawn,' I said under my breath.

Inside the yard I crept past the remains of a '68 Ford and round a pile of dented hub caps. I didn't want Dawn to hear me so I picked my way forward carefully.

I reached the bus and hopped quietly onto the first step. I stopped. I didn't want to go in. I'd been on that bus when it crashed. That terrible crash that I still couldn't remember anything about. But there was no time for that now.

'Gotcha.' I jumped up the next two broken steps into the back of the bus.

Dawn was sitting in the driver's seat with tears in her eyes. 'You,' she spat out. 'Worm Boy. Where's your rotten apple-man?'

She shouldn't have said that. Like I was feeling a bit sorry for her sitting in the very seat where her mother had drowned. But when she rubbished my apple-man I could feel my face burning with anger.

'My Dad gave me that apple-man,' I yelled. 'Don't you – '

She wouldn't even let me finish. 'Your dad, your dad. Don't give me that. Where is he then? What sort of dad goes off and never writes? Never sends a present. Not even a Christmas card. My dad gives you stuff all the time. The only thing you've ever got from yours is a rotten apple.'

I ran down the aisle between the sagging seats and put my face up close to Dawn's. I shouldn't have said what I did. Not when she was sitting right where it happened. But I was really mad. 'What about your mum?' I yelled. 'She wanted to get away from you so bad that she drove the bus off the cliff into the river and drowned. And nearly killed me too.'

Dawn just about exploded. I had really pressed the right buttons. She jumped out of her seat and shoved me onto the floor. The Milo tin rolled down the aisle and the lid popped off. My little apple-man spilled out and lay there like a wizened corpse.

Dawn sat on my chest and pinned my arms to the ground with her knees. I couldn't move. I could hardly breathe. She was much stronger than me. And she knew it.

'I'm going to get your rotten apple-man,' she said. 'And flush it down the dunny.'

I squirmed and heaved but I just couldn't move her. If she wanted to, she could do whatever she liked. I knew that if she ran off with him, I'd never catch her. She was just too fast. It would be the last I'd see of my apple-man.

It's amazing how they make those little apple faces. They get an extra-big apple and let it slowly shrivel up so that it's all wrinkled and dry. They they sew it so that it has little eyes and a mouth and a chin. They make a wooden body and, hey presto – a great little troll with an ugly face.

'Don't touch it,' I screamed. 'I'll kill you.' I bucked

like a horse but she just pressed down harder with her knees.

'It's got worms,' she said. 'Horrible little slobberers.'

I knew that. I twisted my head sideways and looked at them. I was a bit worried when I first saw them. What if they ate the whole apple-head off the doll? Dad would be sad if his present got ruined. The funny thing is, though, the apple-man never changed. The slobberers must have eaten something, but what? They couldn't have been eating the apple or there'd be none left.

My arms were starting to tingle with pins and needles. Dawn's knees were knobbly. 'Give in, Worm Boy,' she said.

'Never,' I said.

So we just stayed there on the floor of the bus. I stared up into her ugly mug and she glared down into mine. I decided not to look at her so I fixed my eyes on a seat where the skeleton of a dead goat sat like a ghostly passenger from the past. How the heck did that get there? It must have wandered in and died.

The image of the skeleton sort of locked itself in my head.

Suddenly Dawn gave a scream and jumped up. She was looking down the aisle at the slobberers. Typical girl. Tough as an ox but scared of a few little grubs.

Then I looked a bit more closely. Oh no. I scrambled up and backed off. The skin of the apple-man had begun to boil. A huge grub erupted from a wrinkled scar on the apple-man's face. It wormed itself out, wriggling, wriggling, wriggling. Tiny veins and purple blood. Little pinpricks of glowing green eyes. Wet fangs and three or four slobbering, sucking tongues coming out of its mouth.

I hadn't seen a slobberer like this before. Maybe they were changing. It crawled towards us followed by another and another and another. Each one the same. It was weird. They slimed out of the apple-man's eyes and ears and hair. Soon there were twenty or thirty. They advanced towards us in lines like an army of little snakes.

'I'm out of here,' shrieked Dawn.

Suddenly the slobberers stopped. They reared up as one and seemed to look about. Then they turned and slithered in panic towards the door.

'Hey,' I yelled. 'Come back. She won't hurt you.'

It seems funny to say this but I didn't want to lose them. Since they had been living in the apple-man I had come to like them even though they were pretty yucky. They were a bit like tenants renting a house. They lived in the apple-man and they didn't really do any harm. And no one else had anything like them.

I grabbed the apple-man and ran outside the bus. The slobberers were lined up some distance away. They stared at the bus and seemed to be making frightened, slurping noises. Their little tongues flickered in and out. Weird. It wasn't Dawn they were frightened of. She had run out and was already climbing through the hole in the fence. Heading for home as quick as her legs could take her. What a chicken.

No, the slobberers weren't scared of Dawn. It was something to do with the bus. To be honest, I thought it was a bit spooky myself.

I walked up close to them and put the apple-man down on the ground. 'Come on, guys,' I said. 'Come home. Come home to Daddy.'

In a flash they streaked across the ground towards the apple-man. They wormed and wriggled and fought each other in their hurry to get back inside. There was a bit of a traffic jam at the nostrils. After a few seconds they were gone. Everything was back to normal. For now anyway.

I picked up my apple-man and headed back to the bus. I went inside and put him back in the Milo tin. No point taking risks. I couldn't take the chance that my little slobberers might escape again. Things were weird enough already.

I jumped out of the bus and walked towards the hole

in the fence. I was glad to be leaving. The slobberers didn't like that bus.

And neither did I.

THREE

Before the wedding I'd been scared three times in my life. Really scared. The sort of scared where people sit you down. Give you hot drinks. Say 'take deep breaths, Dawn' and peek to see if you've wet your pants.

The first time was when I saw Dad crying just before he told me Mum had died.

The second was at Mum's funeral when I heard Mrs Lecter from the newsagents whispering to Mrs Gleeson the librarian. Whispering that Mum had killed herself on purpose.

The third was when Gramps told

me that a rotting beam at the Wilsons' place had crushed a shearer and I thought he meant Dad.

What happened in the bus after the wedding made it four.

I ran out of that wrecker's yard faster than I'd ever run, even faster than I'd run after biting Mrs Lecter at Mum's funeral.

When I got home I threw myself onto my bed. I couldn't stop thinking about it. I couldn't stop shaking. I could still see it, there on the floor of the bus.

Worm Boy probably thought I'd screamed because of the slobberers.

I hadn't. I'd screamed because of the shoe.

It was under the driver's seat. I'd never noticed it before, probably because I'd never had my face that close to the floor before.

It was covered in dust and mildew, but I'd have recognised it anywhere.

Mum's shoe.

She was wearing it the day she died.

Even after five years you don't forget your Mum's favourite bus-driving shoes. Specially when you used to spend so much time spitting on them and polishing them with the tea towel.

It didn't look polished now. It looked twisted and scraped and sad, and it made me think of what Mum's body must have looked like when the police divers pulled her out of the river.

That's why I had to get out of the bus.

I yelled something and pushed past Rory, who was busy with his dopey worms, and jumped out and ran.

All the way home I told myself the shoe wasn't real. It was the stress I'd been under lately. The stress of a wedding and a new step-family and trying to push Rory through the metal floor of a bus. Stress could make you see things, I'd read it in a comic about an alcoholic astronaut.

But when Rory got home, I was still shaking and still seeing that shoe.

'Chicken,' he said, still clutching my Milo tin. 'Scared of a few grubs. Pathetic.'

I should have got him in a neck-lock and grabbed my tin. I almost did. But I knew Mum wouldn't have approved. So instead I took a few deep breaths and told him how in my opinion Tasmanian souvenir manufacturers who use worm-infested apples should be reported to the health authorities.

Then Dad got home and yelled at me for a bit.

'Children do not disrupt their parents' weddings,' he shouted. 'And they go to the reception whether they like it or not.'

Stuff like that.

When he'd calmed down, we talked.

'I know it's not easy, this step-family lark,' said Dad. 'but I want you to give it a go, love, okay?'

I told him I would.

We hugged each other.

While Dad had his arms round me, I saw Rory watching from the doorway. As soon as our eyes met, he turned away. There was something about his expression that made me feel sorry for him. Just for a sec. Until I saw he was still clutching my Milo tin. And I remembered he's got a mum who's perfectly capable of hugging him if she doesn't mind getting a bit of worm poo on her.

Dad launched into making a lamb stew for him and Eileen to take on their honeymoon camping trip, and I helped him.

I like cooking with Dad. Being a shearer, he's best at peeling, so I get to use the cleaver.

Once the stew was bubbling away, we went out onto the back verandah for a lemonade. I almost told Dad about the shoe, but I decided not to. No point in upsetting him. Not on his wedding day.

Dad spotted Rory skulking about in the kitchen.

'Hey, Roars,' he called. 'Want a lemonade?'

Rory jumped guiltily. He'd probably already had about three cans while we weren't looking.

Then Eileen arrived with Gramps.

'That was the best wedding I've ever been to,' said Gramps. He reached into his pocket. 'Anyone want a curried-egg sandwich?'

I was the only one who did.

Then I helped Dad get the camping things together while Eileen and Worm Boy unpacked their moving cartons and got Rory's room straight. Assembled his bed and hung all the little worm clothes in the wardrobe, that sort of stuff.

Soon it was time for Dad and Eileen to go.

I hugged Dad again. Rory hugged his mum. Then there was the tricky bit. I took a deep breath and gave Eileen a quick squeeze. Luckily I'm taller than her so our faces didn't have to touch.

Dad sort of half hugged, half patted Rory.

Gramps kissed everyone.

'Have you got the shovel?' Eileen asked Dad.

I sighed. It didn't seem very romantic. Most people went to Bali or Sydney or some other exotic place for their honeymoon, not camping on Bald Mountain where there weren't any dunnies. Oh well, I thought, it's what they both like.

'Be good kids for Gramps,' yelled Dad. 'See you in three days.'

It felt really strange, watching Dad drive off with

another woman. I mean I'd seen him driving places with Eileen hundreds of times, but this was different because now we were stuck with each other and our lives would never be the same.

The weird stuff started almost straight away.

Gramps said, 'Okay, kids, let's have lunch,' and we had to remind him it was dinner time.

While he and Rory had a look in the freezer, I grabbed the opportunity to get my tin back.

It was sitting on Rory's bedside table. I took the lid off and emptied that ugly little apple-man onto the floor. Its evil-looking eyes peered up at me.

Then I heard a scratching sound. Another pair of eyes was watching me. From the top of the chest of drawers. Rory's mouse in its cage.

I stuck my tongue out at both of them. Mum used to do her sewing and charity book-keeping in that room and nobody else had the right to invade it.

Back in my room I hid the tin in the bottom of my wardrobe under the abseiling ropes Dad gave me for my birthday.

'Don't say a word,' I whispered to Finger, my gold-fish. 'There are invaders in the house and we've got to be on our guard.'

After dinner, while me and Gramps washed up, I took a chance.

'Gramps,' I said, 'have you ever seen a shoe that you thought was there but it actually wasn't?'

Gramps thought about this.

'Once,' he said, 'I didn't see a shoe that I thought wasn't there but it actually was. Work boot, next to my vegie garden, in front of the wheelbarrow. I tripped over it and squashed my sprouts.'

I decided not to continue with the conversation, partly because Gramps was chuckling so loudly, and partly because Rory had stormed into the kitchen, red-faced.

'You stupid idiot,' he shouted. 'You let them out of the tin. Do you have any idea what you've just done?'

'It's my tin,' I said.

'Tin,' said Gramps. 'That's right. I squashed my tobacco tin too.'

Rory rushed out and I finished the drying up. Stupid idiot yourself, I thought. They're only a bunch of worms. If you're that worried about them, train them to come when you whistle.

Then I went to my room.

As soon as I walked in I could feel something was wrong. It took me two seconds to spot it.

Finger, floating at the top of her tank.

Heart pounding, I scooped her out and peered at her gills. She was dead. It must have just happened because she was still loose and floppy.

Even as my eyes filled with tears I felt rage eating into my guts. That vicious mongrel. Just 'cos I let a few of his crummy worms escape, he kills my pet.

Still holding Finger I headed for the door.

That mouse was dead meat.

Rory appeared in the doorway. I decided to pound him first, then do the mouse.

'You killed my – ' I yelled, then stopped because he was yelling too.

And he was holding something out. It looked like a small brown bag. I was confused. Why would a kid who'd just killed my fish think I'd care that he'd found a bag to keep his dopey worms in?

Then I realised it wasn't a bag, it was a mouse.

Rory was sniffing and blinking. He was still angry but I could tell he was upset as well.

'He's ... he's ...' Rory struggled to get the words out.

He didn't need to.

I could see what he was trying to say.

The mouse was dead and it didn't have any bones.

FOUR

I **stormed out of** the kitchen. My head started to swim
with red-hot anger. Dreadful Dawn let my slobberers
out. On purpose. And Mum and Jack had gone off on
their honeymoon and left me in the camp of the enemy.

I went back to my new bedroom (not nearly as good
as my old one) and threw myself onto the bed. I silently
hoped that their marriage would break up as quickly
as possible. Step-families suck. That's what I thought.
I hated Dawn for letting my slobberers out. She was so
stupid.

Gramps was the only decent one. Out of all of them
he was my favourite. He was certainly a
lot better than Big Bad Dawn.

Then I started thinking about Dad.
And remembering.

My dad was handsome. Mum used to
say all the girls were after him but she
was the one who got him.

What I remembered was his kind face.
He was one of those people who always

looked happy. He didn't have a mean bone in his body. Why did he go and leave me?

I tried to push down the tears. 'Don't cry. Don't cry. Be a man.'

I got up and went over to Nibbler's cage to get him out and have a play. He wasn't running around on his wheel like he usually does. He was inside his little wooden nest. I opened the lid and pulled him out.

He was dead.

And flat. And empty. He looked like a tiny possum that had been lying on the road for a couple of weeks. Run over by thousands of cars. Nibbler was stiff and dry. His bones were gone. His innards were gone. His eyes were gone. He was nothing but a flattened dried-up skin.

My little mouse. My friend. The only one in this house who would listen. Gone.

I blinked back my tears.

Dawn. The scumbag. The murderer. She had it coming this time.

I held the remains of Nibbler in my hand and ran out of the room. She was standing there looking at me with hatred in her eyes.

We both shouted the same thing at the same time.

'You killed my – '

Then we stopped. Our mouths hanging open. She

was holding her goldfish and crying. It was shrivelled and horrible with no bones and no innards.

I knew straight away that she hadn't killed Nibbler. She's awful, but she wouldn't kill her own goldfish. Someone else – something else – had killed Nibbler and Finger and sucked all of their bones and innards out.

Dawn's eyes grew rounder and rounder. So did mine. What was going on?

Then she pushed past me into my bedroom. I turned and saw what she saw.

My little apple-man was still on the floor where she had thrown him. Slobberers were wriggling all over him. They were wriggling out of my apple-man at an incredible speed. Twenty or thirty of them. Flickering tongues, evil eyes, pulsing veins. Leeches with tongues. That's what they reminded me of.

They looked at us, then reared up like snakes about to strike. My legs turned to jelly. I felt sick and scared. What were they looking at us like that for? Were they hungry?

If they were, they must have decided that we were a bit too big for them. They slithered out of the window before Dawn or I could even take a breath.

A large magpie sat on the lawn pecking at a piece of bread that Gramps had thrown there. It looked with interest at the approaching slobberers and hopped towards them.

Food.

Well, the magpie was right about that. There was food there all right.

Him.

Horrible, horrible, horrible. The slobberers swarmed all over the poor bird. He gave one squawk and flew into the air just above our heads. The slobberers began to suck. Waving tongues and slurping mouths began to empty him out in front of our eyes. Without a sound the bird and his slimy passengers plummeted onto the grass. Feathers fluttered down slowly.

By the time the last feather had landed the magpie was nothing but an empty, eyeless skin.

The slobberers seemed to have grown after their meal. They were definitely swollen. But that didn't slow them down at all. Before either of us could say a word they had wriggled across the lawn and disappeared under the floor of the garage.

It was the most terrible sight I had ever seen. The slobberers had eaten the magpie alive. Gorging themselves like bloated maggots.

I had to tell Dawn what I had done. Mum and Jack were in terrible danger.

The words stuck in my throat but I managed to get

them out. 'Dawn,' I said. 'I put some slobberers in their stew.'

Dawn turned on me half in fury, half in horror. 'You put them in the stew? My dad's going to eat that.'

'So's my mum.' I could hardly find my voice. 'You tried to stop them getting married. I wanted to bust them up. You know – have a row over the worms. Then Mum and me could go back to our place. And never have to see you and Jack again.'

'You stupid idiot,' Dawn yelled. 'Did you see what they did to that bird?'

Dawn spun round and looked viciously at the apple-man. She took a step towards him and grabbed my cricket bat. I knew what she was going to do. And I knew what I had already done. Putting them in Mum's stew. They were dangerous and we had to get rid of them. But I wasn't going to let Dawn smash up the apple-man. No way.

Dawn lifted the bat and then froze. So did I. There was one slobberer left. A long one. A very long one. It slithered out of the apple-man's left eye. On and on and on. It seemed endless. Like a worm of rotten black toothpaste coming out of a tube.

Dawn screamed and closed her eyes in horror.

I couldn't stop looking at the terrible sight. The slobberer finally left the apple and started to coil and uncoil on the floor. What was it doing?

It was writing. Yes writing. It slowly formed its body into joined-up letters. Letters that spelt out a single word:

karl

'Aagh,' I shrieked.

Dawn opened her eyes. But she had missed seeing the word. The slobberer was wriggling towards the window as fast as it could go. 'Take that,' yelled Dawn. She hurled the bat at the slobberer and it skidded across the floor, narrowly missing the horrible creature's tail. In a flash the slobberer vanished out of the window.

'Come on,' yelled Dawn. 'We have to get to Dad and Eileen before they eat that stew.'

She scrambled out of the door. Out of the house. I grabbed my apple-man and shoved him into my pocket. Then I ran out after her.

'Gramps can help us,' I panted.

Dawn looked at me with contempt. 'Gramps can't even help himself,' she said.

She was right about that. Only an hour before, I had seen Gramps put his electric drill in the freezer. He was definitely past it.

We both looked around. In the garage was Mum's trail bike. As we ran towards it, I knew that Dawn was filled with terrible thoughts about the slobberers and Jack and my mum and what might be happening up on Bald Mountain.

I was just as worried. But I also had another horror to cope with.

The word that the slobberer had spelt out. Karl. That terrible, wonderful word was the name of my father.

FIVE

Stay calm, I said to myself as we sprinted to the garage. Don't panic. When you panic your brain turns into a thickshake.

It wasn't easy.

Dad's overalls and Eileen's bike gear were hanging on the garage wall, saggy and empty like sucked-out skins.

I forced myself to stop imagining things.

28

Rory pushed me out of the way and leapt onto the trail bike.

'Wait,' I said. 'It's too risky. Sergeant Wallace said if he sees you on the street on that bike again he'll use you as lawn fertiliser.'

Rory ignored me and kick-started the engine.

'Okay,' I yelled. 'Seeing as we're going to end up at the police station anyway, let's just go there now and get them to save Dad and Eileen.'

Rory glared at me.

'No,' he shouted. 'No cops.' He turned the engine off and slumped forward onto the handlebars.

I felt sorry for him. When your mum's a courier and she's got as many unpaid speeding tickets as his mum, it doesn't leave you a heap of places to go in an emergency.

I had an idea. I grabbed Eileen's bike jacket off the wall, put it on, grabbed the helmets and threw Rory's to him.

'Shift back,' I said. 'With this stuff on, people'll think I'm your mum. She's almost as big as me.'

I swung my leg over the bike and started it.

'Have you ridden a two-fifty before?' yelled Rory.

'Course,' I replied.

My neck went into a cramp and I had a sudden urge for a curried-egg sandwich. I couldn't understand it.

DAWN

Dad had let me have a go on a sheep bike once and that was almost a two-fifty.

I jerked the bike into gear and we jolted out of the garage.

Standing in the driveway, watching us, was Gramps.

My guts sagged. I hit the brakes and heard Rory give a groan of despair through his helmet.

Gramps stared at me. 'Eileen,' he said. 'I thought you were on your honeymoon.'

I wanted to tear my helmet off and show Gramps it was me. Then I remembered Dad and Eileen with their stew full of slobbering parasites. The trouble with Gramps is that if you start a conversation he gets off the track and ends up talking about woodwork.

I revved the bike and we hurtled out of the driveway in a cloud of dust and magpie feathers. Halfway down the street I felt Rory's helmet bang against mine.

'How long till we get to Bald Mountain?' he shouted.

'About an hour,' I yelled. 'A bit longer if you keep grabbing my shoulders and we crash and we have to go via the hospital.'

Rory put his arms round my waist. It wasn't a great feeling. At the time I'd probably have preferred a slobberer. I told myself to grow up and stop being squeamish.

The trip went pretty well all the way down our street

and round the corner past the library.

Then we had to stop at a red light. I felt Rory stiffen behind me.

'Relax,' I said. 'We'll get there.'

Rory didn't relax. He gave a gasp.

'It's Dad,' he said. 'Over there. Dad.'

He was pointing to a red car on the other side of the road. The windows were tinted and I couldn't see the driver too well, but he certainly looked like the photos I'd seen of Rory's dad.

I blinked and peered and tried to see more clearly.

'Dad,' yelled Rory.

The guy turned and stared at us. Suddenly he didn't look anything like Rory's dad. Rory's dad's face was pretty ordinary and this guy's features were all lop-sided and he had a moustache.

I felt Rory sag behind me.

'I thought it was Dad,' he mumbled.

I could feel his heart thumping in my back.

Poor kid, I thought. At least when a parent's dead you know you'll never see them again. When one just nicks off, you're always hoping.

Which made me think of my dad and whether I'd see him again.

When my eyes had stopped stinging I noticed someone else was staring at us. The bloke in the grey car behind us. He was pretending not to, but I could see his beady eyes in my rear-vision mirror.

It was Mr Kinloch from the Wool Growers' Association. He'd been to our place heaps of times 'cos he and Dad both collected wool samples.

'Get ready for a chase,' I muttered to Rory. 'I think he's recognised my socks.'

My guts clenched and Rory's arms tightened round my waist. I wondered if a bike could go faster than a car. Probably not when the person driving the bike didn't know how to get into fourth gear.

The light turned green.

I revved the bike and we screeched away.

Once the front wheel was back on the ground and my heart was back in my chest, I glanced into the mirror. Mr Kinloch was turning down Station Street.

We headed out of town, me hanging on to the handlebars weak with relief, and Rory hanging on to me muttering about the wear on his mother's tyres.

We didn't know it then, but they were about to get even more worn.

It started when we were out on Bald Mountain Road. I'd just got the hang of fourth gear and we were rocketing along. Rory's helmet clunked against mine again.

'Stop the bike,' he shouted. 'Don't look down.'

His voice had the same fake squeaky fear he'd used in the school play when he was a dying general. His acting hadn't been real good then either.

'Stow it, peabrain,' I yelled, and carried on trying to find fifth gear.

That's all I need, I thought, Worm Boy playing stupid tricks to get his own back for the wheelie at the traffic lights. Has the cretin forgotten this is an emergency?

I found fifth.

'Stop!' screamed Rory. He wasn't acting.

Then I saw it. Crawling out of the hollow handlebar where the stopper had fallen off.

The biggest slobberer yet.

It was the size of a human poo and I could see its wet veiny body pulsing and its slimy tongues darting and its green eyes glaring.

I screamed and took my hand off the handlebar. The bike wobbled and started to slow down.

The slobberer slimed its way along the metal and flopped onto my jacket.

I screamed again.

Others were following it. Slithering out of the handlebar and dropping onto me. Crawling up my chest.

I tried to knock them off. My bike glove slapped against slobbery rubbery muscle. They didn't budge.

DAWN

Their angry eyes just got bigger and glared up at me.

It was like they'd noticed me for the first time.

They started jabbing their tongues into my vinyl jacket. I almost fainted. I waited for them to suck me dry like the magpie.

Then I noticed the tongues were stabbing into the vinyl but not going all the way through.

Relief flooded through me.

'Look out!' yelled Rory.

Suddenly I realised we weren't on the road any more. Branches and leaves were whipping my face and the bike was airborne.

Then we were through the scrub and in the clear, crashing down, the bike on its side, skidding in a shower of dirt and twigs towards a huge sheet of metal.

Metal?

No, water.

I let go of the bike.

As I rolled painfully over grass tussocks and dried sheep droppings and Rory's knees, I heard a loud splash.

As soon as I stopped rolling I tore the jacket off. I checked every centimetre of it and my whole shaking body. Only then did I see that, like the slobberers, the bike had vanished.

Just ripples on the surface of a large dam.

'Great,' yelled Rory, his voice cracking. He had a cut on his face. 'Now we'll never save them. You're as hopeless as your mother.'

I was shaking so much I could hardly get my hands into fists. But I managed it.

And I'd have managed to pound them into his sneering mouth if I hadn't seen the sun glinting off something way down the hill, past the lower paddock, on Ravine Road.

The windscreen of a car. A parked car. A yellow car with a blue door, which was the only one the wrecker had available after Mal Gleeson backed into us at the speedway.

Dad's car.

Getting down there took a while because we were both limping.

By the time we got close it was almost dusk. The car was half in shadow and at first I couldn't see inside.

All I could see was that the front doors were wide open. The engine was running. The bonnet was crumpled against a tree.

Nothing seemed to be slithering over the car. Not on the outside anyway.

'Dad,' I yelled.

DAWN

'Mum,' yelled Rory.

No answer.

Sobs wanted to come out of my throat. I didn't let them.

Rory handed me a long stick. He was holding one too, like a spear. 'Thanks,' I said, grateful that even cretins have good ideas sometimes.

We looked at each other, then crept towards the car.

Inside the car was the most revolting thing I'd ever seen.

Splattered over the seats, floor, dashboard and roof.

Lamb stew.

Holding our breath, we prodded the lumps of meat and the globs of soggy potato and the dripping upholstery with our spears.

No slobberers.

And no Dad and Eileen.

SIX

They must be dead. Mum and Jack.

That's all I could think when I saw the mangled car. I had to look in that car – but what would I find? Smashed and crushed bodies? I stared inside. Lamb stew was splattered everywhere. There was blood on the seats. But the car was empty. With trembling hands I reached in through the driver's open door and turned off the ignition.

Frantically Dawn and I started to search through the bushes. My legs didn't want to go but I forced them forwards. I didn't know what we were going to find. It could have been the most awful thing ever. Your worst nightmare.

No. Don't think it. Put it out of your mind. Mum and Jack might be lying there under the bushes. Scared but okay. Smiling and glad to see us. That's what I told myself anyway. That's what I hoped for.

We ran from bush to bush shouting wildly.

'Mum.'

'Dad.'

'Mum.'

'Dad.'

'Mum.'

'Dad.'

In the end I didn't find my worst nightmare. I found my second worst.

They were gone.

'Murderer,' screamed Dawn. 'You put those stinking worms in the stew. They must have come out. Like on the bike. And now what's happened. They probably – '

'Stop,' I yelled. 'Stop, stop, stop.' I put my hands over my ears. I didn't want to hear the next bit. I was trying not to think about the sucked-out fish. And the mouse. And the magpie.

'They're still alive,' I said, hoping – oh, hoping so badly that I was right.

'How do you know?' Dawn shrieked.

My voice came out in a scratchy whisper. 'No skins.'

Dawn fell silent.

Everything fell silent.

In the surrounding bush there was not a sound. Not the croak of a frog or the call of a bird. Not the rub of a cricket's legs. Not even the sound of a leaf falling to the rocky ground.

The whole forest was frozen with terror.

We whispered. Not knowing why.

'I'm going to the cops,' said Dawn.

'No,' I hissed. 'I think my dad's involved with this.'

'What's he got to do with it?' she said. 'That wasn't him back in town.'

I couldn't tell her about the worm spelling out Dad's name. I just couldn't. So I said nothing.

Dawn and I faced each other in the silent twilight.

Until . . .

A sound. Far off. A soft, fearful whooshing. Coming from somewhere off to the left. A slushing, slurping noise. Like a hose in reverse. Sucking up water.

A cold shiver ran over my skin. We stared at each other for a fraction of a second. And then, trying not to scream, we both started scrambling up to the road the way we had come.

We reached the road and started to run downhill. If only a car would come.

My bad leg slowed me down and Dawn disappeared round a bend. She could run so much faster than me even with her bruised leg. Why didn't she wait? Did she hate me that much?

A sudden shriek filled the air. Oh no. I didn't want Dawn for a step-sister, but right then, in the middle of all that terror, she was a million times better than no one.

I rounded the corner and found her staring at a flat dead skin on the road.

'A possum,' Dawn yelled.

'Flattened by a car,' I panted hopefully.

'I wish,' said Dawn.

We crouched down over the possum. It was still warm. No bones or innards. Not even any blood. Slobberers.

We stared down the road into the growing darkness. 'They must be close,' I gasped.

The slurping, slushing, sucking was growing louder, ahead of us and behind us.

'There's only one way to go,' I yelled. 'Down there.' I plunged off the road and into the dense bush. Dawn crashed behind me without a word.

Maybe we would shake them off. Maybe they would rush past our trail and down the road. That was the hope that filled my mind as night began to fall. That was the hope that kept me going. Down, down, down. Clambering over logs. Stumbling. Bleeding from grazed knees and elbows.

Slurp, slurp, slurp.

Oh no. They hadn't rushed past. They hadn't been fooled. They were somewhere behind us now, not far back in the darkness. Loose, wet tongues slithering into every crack and crevice. Following our trail like boneless bloodhounds. Dragging their hungry bellies over the ground.

Fear. Fear was numb inside me like a lump of ice. I could tell by the growing noise of the slurps that the slobberers were getting closer.

There were so many things to think about. So many questions. But only one that really mattered at that moment.

How were we going to escape?

We ran and jumped and fell. But all the time, in the gum trees, somewhere behind, always within earshot, *slobber, slobber, slobber. Slurp, slurp, slurp.*

'They're going to catch us,' said Dawn. She grasped her spear tightly. 'We'll have to fight them.'

'Don't be mad,' I said. 'You saw that sucked-out possum. How would you like – ?' In the moonlight I saw her face crumple and stopped in mid-sentence.

'Maybe they won't attack in the night,' she said.

I gave a snort. 'I don't think so,' I said. 'Look.'

Not far behind, dozens of glowing green specks blinked through the black trees.

Eyes.

Eyes were seeking us out. The slobberers could see in the dark. I was sure of it.

We crashed onwards in blind panic. My sides ached and my bad leg was hurting. Ever since Dawn's mum had driven me and that bus into the river I couldn't walk or run properly. My knee was killing me.

But it wasn't far to the bottom of the gully. I had a plan. Desperate, but it might work. Dawn was stronger. Dawn was bigger. Dawn was faster. But I was smarter. That's what I thought at the time anyway.

'There,' I said as we burst out of the trees. 'The river. We must be close to the Wilsons' jetty.'

We stumbled along the river bank.

There it was. A small dinghy tied up to a tree. With not so much as a word to each other we jumped in. Dawn untied the rope without even being asked and I pushed us into the centre of the stream. The bank was just dark shadows. Not even a glimmer of moonlight.

But through the gloom it was not hard to see our nightmare. Green glowing eyes. Dozens of them. Staring out into the river from the receding bank.

The current was strong and we drifted downstream quickly. The eyes blinked, growing smaller as we moved away. Soon they were only little pinpricks. Like a bank of unfriendly glow-worms in the dark.

Relief flooded through me. We were leaving the slobberers behind. 'You know what?' I screamed into the night. 'You guys suck.' I laughed hoarsely.

Dawn started to laugh with me. Hysterical laughter.

At that very moment the eyes went out. Yes, I swear it was the exact moment we laughed. Just as if someone had thrown a switch.

'We'll call the cops,' said Dawn. 'They'll get the army. They'll wipe them out with flame-throwers or snail-killer or something.'

This time I said nothing about Dad and the cops. We were safe for now but I had a feeling that the slobberers or the apple-man or some other nameless thing was not going to let us tell anyone. I wondered what lay ahead. Waiting in the dark.

'They might be able to swim,' I said.

'Then why didn't they jump into the river after us?'

'Maybe they're going to cut us off somewhere.'

We both shuddered.

'There must be somewhere we can hide,' I said. 'The water will be covering our trail.'

Dawn didn't answer. She was funny like that. Sometimes it was really hard to know what was going on in her weird mind. She was probably thinking everything was my fault.

As we drifted silently in the darkness my thoughts

turned to Dad. He gave me that apple-man.

Was Dad behind all this? Was he a crook? Why did he and Mum bust up? Just because he had gone off didn't mean he'd stopped loving me. Did it?

I didn't care. I loved him. He was still my dad no matter what he might have done. He couldn't have sent the slobberers. Not to suck out his own son. Dad's face floated into my mind. His kind, laughing face. The one that watched me so proudly when I rode my dirt bike. The one who always called me mate and told weird jokes.

I missed him.

I thought about how Mum had taken all of Dad's photos out of the family album. She said she didn't want to hurt Jack's feelings. But what about mine? All I had to remind me of Dad was my little apple-man in my pocket. And the slobberers. Had they been part of Dad's present? Nah, they couldn't be. They killed animals. They were dangerous.

Why had Dad gone, leaving just me and Mum?

I didn't even have *her* to myself. She had fallen in love with Jack. Then I really only had half a Mum.

And now I had no Mum at all. She was gone. Dead for all I knew. Unless I could find her.

And how could I do that? I was only a boy.

I cried silently and hoped that Dawn couldn't see my tears in the night.

SEVEN

I cried silently and hoped that Rory couldn't see my tears in the night.

Oh, Dad. Please. Not you too.

If Dad was dead, there was just me.

Well, as good as.

I tried to imagine life with Gramps and Worm Boy. One person who didn't know which planet I was on and one who didn't care.

As I stared at the black water swirling round the little boat, another awful thought wormed its way into my guts.

Perhaps we were cursed. A horrible family curse that Mum and Dad didn't know anything about. Perhaps one of our ancestors did something really bad and as a result two wonderful people had to die in the prime of life. With all their teeth. With hardly any wrinkles. With sparkling eyes that could spot me pinching a biscuit from a hundred metres . . .

I made myself stop.

DAWN

Don't give up, that was Dad's motto. In my head I could hear him. 'Don't give up till you've searched the back paddock.' It was an old farmer's saying he used when a mob of sheep or a can-opener went missing.

Don't worry, Dad, I said silently. I'll find you if I have to search every back paddock in Australia.

'Aaghhh!'

Worm Boy was yelling.

Our boat was drifting close to the river bank. Overhanging branches were nearly taking our heads off.

'Push,' he shouted.

We rammed the oars into the roots and heaved ourselves back out into the main current. Rory peered anxiously into the dark trees.

'That was close,' he panted. 'We're lucky we didn't end up with a boat full of slobberers.'

He looked so small and frail and anxious sitting there, eyes big in the moonlight. Suddenly I wanted to make him feel better.

'Don't be a dope,' I said. 'We're miles downstream. Slobberers can't travel that fast.'

Oh, how wrong I was.

How very very dead wrong.

Even as I was pretending to roll my eyes at Worm Boy's dopeyness, I saw the green specks of light overhead.

Not in the trees.

In the black sky.

I must have gasped. Rory saw them too. We stared up, gripping the sides of the boat.

'They're just stars,' I said. 'They just look green 'cos of atmospheric conditions.'

I wanted to believe it, but my neck was killing me and I would have crawled over sheep's poo for a curried-egg sandwich.

'They're moving,' croaked Rory. 'I think they're watching us.'

'As if,' I said. 'Slobberers can't fly.'

Wrong again.

Something splashed into the water.

I gripped my oar as hard as my shaking hands would let me, ready to make slobberer schnitzel. But it wasn't a green-eyed slime-slug floating next to the boat.

It was a fruit bat.

I turned it over with my oar.

A big dead fruit bat without a bone or blood vessel in its flat floppy carcass.

We stared at it.

More splashes further down the river.

Suddenly I heard wings beating overhead and realised what was going on. 'The slobberers are flying in on bats,' I yelled, 'and sucking them dry when they want to come down.'

We looked at each other, then peered frantically into the black water. There they were. Slimy torpedoes with green eyes. Speeding away from us.

'Why aren't they attacking?' said Rory.

'Dunno,' I said. 'They must have another plan.' Up ahead, more splashes.

Rory groaned. 'There's a bridge before we reach town.'

'So?' I said.

'So have you ever seen a spider drop off a roof?'

My guts clenched. We rounded a bend. In the distance, friendly street lights. I went weak with relief. Then I saw it. Spanning the river ahead. An arc of green lights. A miniature Sydney Harbour Bridge at night.

'Row,' screamed Rory. 'Row for the bank.'

We thrashed the water with our oars. When the boat rammed into the bank we leapt out, slipping on mud and grabbing at tree trunks.

Tree trunks supporting a canopy of dark branches.

And an army of evil green eyes.

'Run,' yelled Rory.

'Where to?' I shouted as we ploughed through dry grass.

Behind us I could hear the horrible thud, thud, thud of soft things hitting the ground.

'Dunno,' shouted Rory. 'Yes I do.' He veered to our

left, towards Dead Cow Clearing. 'The bus. The slobberers are terrified of the bus.'

I knew how they felt. For several hours I'd been feeling sick every time I thought about Mum's shoe on the bus. I kept having a crazy thought. Drunk people lost their shoe. Mad people. What if the things people said about Mum and the accident were true?

Now, as the jagged iron fence of the wrecker's yard loomed out of the darkness, I knew I couldn't go back on that bus.

'Not the bus,' I pleaded, 'Somewhere else.'

'There isn't anywhere else,' yelled Rory, wide-eyed and frantic.

'There's a caretaker at night,' I said. 'He might have a gun.'

'He's even older than Gramps. He'll think we're burglars and blow our heads off.'

We reached the fence. I glanced back across the moonlit paddock. Green eyes were coming. Slimy bodies hissing over the long dry grass. Tongues slobbering.

I froze.

They were getting bigger.

I stared, terror thudding in my head at their swollen bodies.

'Okay,' I whispered desperately. 'The bus.'

I hurried along the fence, Rory close behind. I tried not to look at the bus standing wrecked and rusting in the yard.

We reached my secret entrance.

'Hurry,' said Rory. 'They're getting closer.'

I couldn't hurry. I couldn't even move. The hole in the fence had gone. Someone had nailed a sheet of iron over it.

There was no way in.

EIGHT

There was no way in to the wrecker's yard. The fence was just too high.

Dawn and I searched around desperately for something – anything that might get us over the top. 'Ah ha,' I shouted. 'Just the thing. A big oil drum.'

I rolled it over to the fence and stood it up on its end. 'You first,' I managed to gasp.

They were coming. They were coming. The slobberers were coming. And they were bigger than ever. Maybe the darkness would hide us. Maybe they would lose our trail. Maybe their horrible, horrible tongues would not pick up our scent.

Maybe.

The top of the fence had been cut to form sharp points. Dawn scrambled onto the drum and pulled the sleeves of her jumper down over her hands. Then she hoisted herself over the razor points in one bound. I heard her land on the other side of the fence. How did she do that? She was so fit.

I couldn't even get onto the oil drum. It rocked from side to side every time I tried to haul myself up.

Slurp, slurp, slurp.

'Aagh. Someone help. Someone come. Anyone.'

'Rory, hurry up.' Dawn's urgent whisper seemed like thunder in my ears.

'Shhh,' I said. 'They'll hear you.' Finally I managed to get onto the drum. I knelt there on my knocking knees. The drum trembled, threatening to upend itself and me onto the hard ground. Carefully I rose to my feet. I pulled my sleeves down over my fingers and gingerly felt the sharp edges of the iron fence.

Slurp, slurp, slurp.

'Aw, gees. Aaghh . . .' The drum skidded off beneath me leaving me dangling by my hands. The steel points of the fence cut through my sweater, scraping the skin off my fingers. I hauled myself up and felt the jagged points tear along my legs. Blood spilled down the fence in a sticky trail.

Slurp, slurp, slurp.

I dropped to the ground inside the wrecker's yard, a bloody bundle of terror spread-eagled on the oily ground. I groaned in pain as I saw Dawn run towards the bus.

Over in his little office the caretaker looked up and scowled. I could see his face glowing dimly in the light of a desk lamp. His dog was curled up by the open door. It gave a low growl and lifted its head.

'My fingers,' I groaned. I held up my cut hands and stared in horror at the blood pouring down my arm. The pain was terrible.

I looked down at my knee. Something inside me seemed to die. Suddenly I didn't care any more. I was like a wounded soldier wanting to be put out of his misery by a friend's bullet.

It was all too much, the running, the pain, the terror. Let them come. Let them come.

I didn't care any more.

Maybe I was slipping into unconsciousness. Just like after the bus crashed. Then I felt something soft and soothing wipe the blood from my left hand. Like a nurse gently wiping a patient's wound. For a second I couldn't take it in. A long, wet, veined tongue slid through a hole in the iron fence. It slithered over my injured fingers, licking up the blood.

A slobberer's tongue. A horrible blue tongue was feasting, slurping, sliming over me. It slid up and touched my face.

I froze. I couldn't move. On the other side of the fence I heard horrible gobbling squeals as the other monsters fought over the bloody trail I had left behind on the fence.

'Aagh.' I tore my hand away and fled after Dawn towards the bus. I snatched a glance over my shoulder. Hideous slobbering tongues, like the tentacles of a monstrous sea anemone, were waving over the top of the fence. Some were pausing at the sharp points. Some were even licking the patches of blood on the spikes.

'Aarf, aarf, aarf.' The caretaker's dog had sensed us. He stood barking, staring into the gloom.

Dawn had reached the bus. 'Rory,' she called. 'I can't go back in there . . .'

'You have to,' I yelled.

Dawn looked over her shoulder. The dog charged towards her. Its lips pulled back over terrible teeth. Growling and howling it leapt. With a scream Dawn ran into the darkness. But the dog wasn't after her. It hurled itself at the gate, springing furiously up at the blue-veined, slithering tongues of the slobberers.

I started up the steps and stumbled. There was something there. Something alive – wedged on the step and blocking the door. A sheep. A stupid sheep. I grabbed it wildly and pulled. My cut finger went right up its wet nose. Oh yuck, yuck, yuck.

As I wrestled with the sheep the caretaker ran out to see what the barking was about. His pot belly jiggled up and down as he lurched across the compound. I stared out from the steps. The moon shone on my face. The caretaker stared right at me and carried on. He must have seen me. But he ran right past. And I couldn't see Dawn anywhere.

The sheep gave one loud baa and scampered off into the night.

Suddenly the gate fell and an army of enormous slobberers poured into the yard. The first slobberer lunged forward and closed its mouth over the dog's jaws.

It shoved its tongue straight down the poor animal's throat. There was a horrible sucking noise like the sound a bath makes as the last of the water drains out. Then the dog collapsed, boneless on the wet ground. It shook for a moment, still alive. A furry handbag of jelly. Its legs no more than quivering ropes.

The dog's eyes rolled for a second and then closed. There was a gurgle and it lay still.

I gave a shudder. For the dog's sake I hoped it was dead.

The caretaker fled howling into the night. Most of the slobberers ignored him. They had other prey. It was me they wanted. But one big grey brute turned and rumbled after the caretaker. It looked like a seal galloping forward into battle.

In the darkness there was a yell. Then silence.

The other slobberers surged in my direction. Fighting with their tongues for the red drops I had left behind me.

They tasted the trail and followed.

Was there anything that could help me? Anything at all? The only thing I had with me was the apple-man. Squashed down in my pocket. With bleeding fingers I pulled him out and stared at him.

My head swam. It felt as if it was filled with a million bees.

RORY

I scrambled into the bus and collapsed.

I was alone.

Outside, somewhere in the darkness, I heard a girl scream.

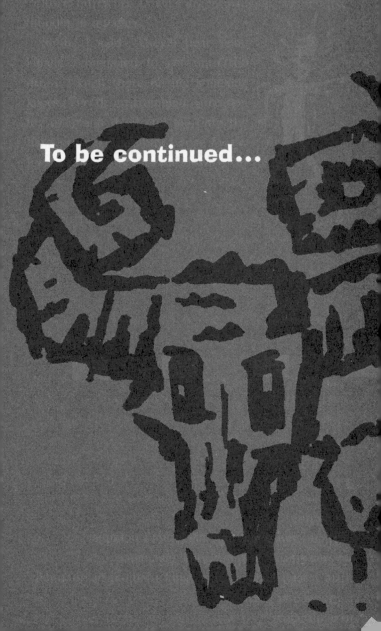

To be continued...

The electrifying six-part serial continues next month...

'I froze. Several slobberer-sized shapes were watching me. Then a cloud shifted off the moon and I saw it was just a mob of sheep. They had weird expressions on their faces, though. Must be an imported breed, I thought, with unusual bones.

'The sheep turned and trotted off. Then stopped and looked back at me. Then trotted some more. Then looked back again...

'I thought I heard a strange sound. No, it couldn't be. Sheep didn't laugh...'

Can Rory and Dawn get it together to find their missing parents? What hope have they got when they are still sworn enemies? Especially when Rory is trapped in the bus and Dawn has run off into the night.

And will they escape the slobberers?

If you want to find out
what happens next, you can
read it in

Wicked!

Part Two
BATTERING RAMS

Sucking you in deeper...

**Coming soon to a
bookstore
near you!**

ThE AuTHoRS

Paul Jennings & Morris Gleitzman are Australia's most popular writers for children. They are also very good friends.

Now, for the first time, they are writing together. Twice as weird, twice as funny, twice as spooky, twice as mind-blowing. If you loved their books before, you'll love <u>Wicked!</u> twice as much.

There's never been anything like it.

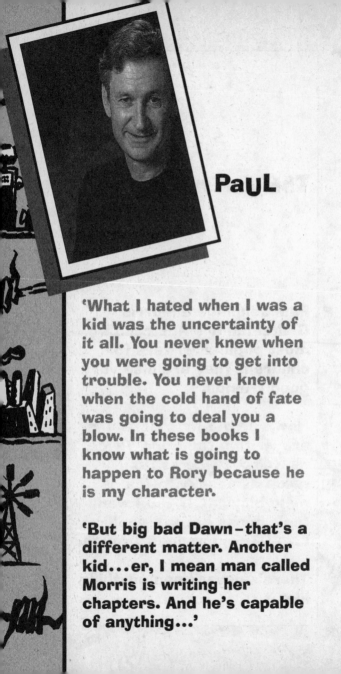

PaUL

'What I hated when I was a kid was the uncertainty of it all. You never knew when you were going to get into trouble. You never knew when the cold hand of fate was going to deal you a blow. In these books I know what is going to happen to Rory because he is my character.

'But big bad Dawn – that's a different matter. Another kid...er, I mean man called Morris is writing her chapters. And he's capable of anything...'

MoRriS

'Almost anything. I couldn't be untidy. Not <u>really</u> untidy, like putting my white shirts on black hangers.

'And I couldn't be wicked. Not <u>really</u> wicked, like running off and leaving a kid to have his bones sucked out by giant worms.

'Not unless I was writing it in a book.'